NO ROOSTERS IN THE DESERT

A Play Based on Fieldwork
by Anna Ochoa O'Leary

by

Kara Hartzler

<u>*NoPassport Press*</u>
Dreaming the Americas Series

No Roosters in the Desert
Copyright 2010 by Kara Hartzler.

This publication is made possible by Borderlands Theater in
collaboration with NoPassport Press. Book Design: Caridad
Svich and Patricia Guzman.

Artwork/Graphic Design for No Roosters in the Desert program:
Landscape photo by Michael Hyatt, Skeleton art by Enrique Rocha,
Digital art by Lori Lieber Graphic Design, Inc.
Artwork for the cover of Arizona: No Roosters in the Desert
Photo: Michael Hyatt, Skeleton art: Enrique Rocha
Cast photo and montage: Andres Volovsek

NoPassport Press: Dreaming the Americas Series
First edition 2010 by NoPassport Press
PO Box 1786, South Gate, CA 90280 USA; NoPassportPress@aol.com
ISBN: 978-0-578-07047-6

No Roosters in the Desert

Development History

No Roosters in the Desert by Kara Hartzler, field work by Anna Ochoa O'Leary PhD. was commissioned by Borderlands Theater, Tucson, Arizona, in 2008 with seed money from the University of Arizona Bi-National Migration Institute. Hartzler, a playwright and immigration attorney for the Florence Immigration Project, Florence, Arizona, used 130 interviews of migrant women border Crossers conducted in 2007/08 by Ms. O'Leary. These interviews were undertaken for the purpose of studying the intersection of mass migrations from Mexico and Central America, increasingly of women, and U.S. border enforcement policies. In addition to these interviews, developed into a fictionalized framework, are indigenous stories inspired by published indigenous texts she encountered while living and working for human rights organizations in Chiapas and Central America. Readings during the development process were held at the Unicorn Theater, Kansas City, LARK Play Development Center, (New York); El Circulo Teatral Mexico City (World Theater Day) and the University of Arizona. Additional funding for development, production and community engagement has been provided by The National Endowment for the Arts, Access to Excellence; The Edgerton Foundation New American Play Award; The National New Play Network, and The Tucson/Pima Arts Council: Kresge Arts Tucson.

Production History

The first of Three Rolling World Premieres, supported in part by the National New Play Network (NNPN), occurred on August 6, 2010 at El Circulo Teatral, in Spanish translation by Eva Zorillo Tessler and Andres Volovsek; Victor Carpinteiro and Alberto Estrell producers (Barclay Goldsmith Associate Producer). Rocio Belmont, Director, with Olga Gottwald, Adriana Resendez, Mikaela Lobos and Jenifer Moreno; original music by Rodney Steve, Lighting and Scenic Design by Monica Kubli. The second world premier: Borderlands Theater, October 7, 2010 in English and community readings in Spanish, Barclay Goldsmith (Artistic Director) directed with Eva Zorillo Tessler, Annabelle Nunez, Veronica del Cerro , Anel Schmidt, Rebeca Cartes (Musician). Scenic and Lighting design by Monica Kubli. The third World Premiere: February 13, 2011, Prop Thtr, Chicago, in English and Spanish, Scott Vehill, Artistic Director and Stefan Brun, Associate Artistic Director, Tanya Saracho, director.

About the Author

Kara Hartzler received her law degree and MFA in Playwriting from the University of Iowa. She is currently the Legal Director at the Florence Immigrant and Refugee Rights Project in Florence, Arizona. Her plays have been produced in New York, Los Angeles, Mexico City, and various other locations.

CAST

MARCELA – *a woman from Guadalajara, early 50's*
ALEJANDRA – *a woman from Mexico City, mid-20's*
GUADALUPE – *a woman from Guatemala, mid-30's*
LUISA – *a woman from Chiapas, Mexico, late teens*

Various INTERVIEWERS, *played by designated cast members*

TIME

Present.

PLACE

A remote border area between Arizona and Mexico and a small interview room.

No Roosters in the Desert

(Sounds of the desert at night, the wind, insects. The lights barely rise to reveal the shadowy outline of four figures frozen in place. Silence.)

GUADALUPE: *(Whisper.)* Do you hear it?

MARCELA: What?

GUADALUPE: That sound. The breathing.

(Silence.)

MARCELA: I don't hear it.

GUADALUPE: Slow, husky. In and out. Like this.

(She demonstrates. Pause.)

There! Do you hear it?

MARCELA: No.

ALEJANDRA: I do.

(Tense silence.)

GUADALUPE: Someone's here.

MARCELA: Where?

GUADALUPE: Just ahead and to the right.

ALEJANDRA: I hear it behind us.

GUADALUPE: There too?

(Silence.)

ALEJANDRA: Do we run?

GUADALUPE: Which way? They're everywhere!

MARCELA: Don't run. If you run, they beat you.

(Clears throat. In a loud voice:)

Hello!

(No answer.)

We're here! We're not going to run.

(Silence.)

You can come get us.

(Silence.)

Hello?

GUADALUPE: I still hear it.

ALEJANDRA: Is it robbers?

MARCELA: We don't have anything to steal.

GUADALUPE: (Ominous.) Maybe they don't want money.

MARCELA: Hello!

(Pause.)

We know you're there. What do you want?

ALEJANDRA: (Chanting.) It's OK; it's going to be OK.

GUADALUPE: I want to see my children. I want to see my babies one more time.

MARCELA: I don't know what you want. But come out and stop scaring us.

(Pause.)

9

We're not doing anything. We just want to pass.

ALEJANDRA: Don't hurt us! Leave us alone!

MARCELA: Hello! HELLO?

> *(Silence. The small sound of a cowbell.*
> *MARCELA begins laughing.)*

GUADALUPE: What is it?

LUISA: It's cows.

GUADALUPE: Are you sure?

LUISA: Yes.

ALEJANDRA: Oh my god.

GUADALUPE: You're sure it's cows?

LUISA: Yes.

MARCELA: (Still laughing uncontrollably.) No, no, it's not just cows, it's Migra Cows!

> *(Sound of several cowbells.)*

GUADALUPE: I thought I was going to die.

ALEJANDRA: *You're fine. We're all fine.*

MARCELA: *We're not fine, this is serious! We've got to deal with the Migra Cows! Get out your passports and visas, they want to inspect them!*

GUADALUPE: *Stop it.*

MARCELA: *You haven't heard? They don't have enough Border Patrol so they're deputizing the cows. Spreading them out along the border. "Can I see your documents, ma'am? MOO!"*

ALEJANDRA: *(Wandering off.) Where are they?*

(LUISA starts to giggle.)

GUADALUPE:*(To LUISA.) Don't laugh at her, we almost died!*

MARCELA: *From what? Death by milking?*

(LUISA laughs. MARCELA approaches one of the cows, holding out her hand.)

Please sir, here's my visa, I know it's expired but I just need to come to your wonderful country and scrub your floors so my little one won't starve. What's that? Only if I give you some hay in return? Oh sir, please have mercy, I don't have any hay on me. What? "Get out now, pinche Mexicana?"

(Turns to LUISA and MARCELA in amazement.)

Even their cows hate us.

(GUADALUPE finally bursts out laughing, followed by LUISA and MARCELA. After a moment, LUISA looks up. We hear a dull thud.)

LUISA: Alejandra?

(No answer.)

ALEJANDRA?

(Lights down on desert and rise on the interview area — a small table with two chairs. The Interviewer can perhaps have a legal pad and wear a scarf or a pair of glasses to distinguish her from her other character.)

(MARCELA is being interviewed by the actor who plays GUADALUPE.)

MARCELA: It was silly. But I need silly sometimes, you know? I think we all do. Have you ever noticed that the poor tell more jokes than the rich? The rich take themselves too seriously, they actually have a chance of winning at life and they want to make good on it. But the poor know they're screwed from the beginning. They know they're going to suffer, it's just when and how much. So they laugh. When there's nothing else to do, you laugh.

(Pause.)

When my husband was going crazy, he thought I was trying to poison him. Every meal he'd stand there in the kitchen while I was cooking and watch me. I had to show him everything I was using, every bean, every pepper, every onion, every grain of salt. He even accused me of feeding the chickens something so they'd lay poison eggs. After a while I thought I was going crazy too. I asked him, "Why would I try to poison you?" He said, "So you can rob me and take all our possessions." I looked at him and said, "What possessions?" I started laughing. "Look around this house. What things could I steal? What do we have?" I was laughing so hard I was crying, and he stared at me with a hurt look on his face. That's the day I stopped going crazy and decided to head north. To try and suffer a little less.

(Pause.)

I've done things. I take responsibility. But that trip, you know, we all did the best we could. We put one foot in front of the other and asked God for help with the next. And sometimes it wasn't only suffering. A few times we laughed.

(Lights down on interview. The deafening sound of a helicopter. A searchlight sweeps across the stage. The sound of a voice as though it's coming through a megaphone.)

VOICE OVER MEGAPHONE: This is the United States Bureau of Customs and Border Protection. Stay where you are. Do not run. Do not run and you will not be harmed. Stay where you are.

(The stage is filled with the commotion of people running in every direction. The sound of horses galloping. Finally the noise dies down and the searchlight disappears. Long silence.)

(We see the shadowy outline of ALEJANDRA picking her way across the stage.)

ALEJANDRA: Hello? Is anyone still here?

(Pause.)

Hello?

MARCELA: *We're here.*

*(MARCELA and GUADALUPE emerge.
GUADALUPE is limping.)*

ALEJANDRA: *(Excitedly.) I was behind that rock. I heard their footsteps go right by but they didn't see me. They were — I can't believe they didn't see me. Where were you?*

MARCELA: *Down in that bank.*

ALEJANDRA: *(To GUADALUPE.) What happened?*

GUADALUPE: *I tripped. Oh, my ankle, it's broken!*

MARCELA: *It's not broken.*

GUADALUPE: *I'm sure it is.*

ALEJANDRA: *Are they gone?*

MARCELA: *They filled up two trucks. I think they got everyone else.*

ALEJANDRA: *Can you walk?*

GUADALUPE: *(As she's walking.) No.*

ALEJANDRA: How did they find us?

MARCELA: They probably —

GUADALUPE: That group was too big. The guides didn't know what they were doing; you can't take a group that big.

MARCELA: I was in a group that big once and —

GUADALUPE: A waste of my money! How am I going to get another two thousand? I'm going to tell them they better get me there for free next —

MARCELA: (Staring across the stage.) There's someone here.

(Silence.)

GUADALUPE: Is it migra?

(LUISA slowly walks across the stage towards them. She wears a huipil and is clutching several tortillas in her hand.)

ALEJANDRA: Are you OK?

(LUISA doesn't answer.)

MARCELA: Did you hide?

(Silence.)

GUADALUPE: *You still have your tortillas.*

LUISA: *I can't lose them.*

MARCELA: *You didn't.*

LUISA: *I hear that if you get catch, they make you to throw them away.*

MARCELA: *They do.*

LUISA: *I hid. And then I start to eat fast as I could so they stay with me safe. They don't go to garbage.*

(Silence.)

GUADALUPE: *So what do we do now?*

ALEJANDRA: *We have to keep going, right? What else would we do?*

GUADALUPE: *I can't walk.*

MARCELA:*(Becoming exasperated.) It's not broken.*

GUADALUPE: *How much longer?*

ALEJANDRA: We're almost there, aren't we?

MARCELA: Probably.

ALEJANDRA: Have any of you crossed before?

(GUADALUPE shakes her head. LUISA doesn't respond.)

MARCELA: This is my third time. I think we should keep going. We have to.

GUADALUPE: Who's going to get us there? We don't know which direction to go.

MARCELA: I think it's that way.

(She points.)

Those mountains look familiar. I think if we stay to the left of them we'll see Tucson.

GUADALUPE: I'll wait here for the migra.

MARCELA: We don't know when the migra's coming back. It could be days, it could be weeks. You can't stay here by yourself.

GUADALUPE: My ankle hurts.

ALEJANDRA: We'll go slow. You can make it!

GUADALUPE: *Just leave me here.*

MARCELA: *We're not going to leave you. We're not leaving anyone.*

ALEJANDRA: *We can call; tell them you're here.*

(Looking at cell phone. To LUISA.)

Are you getting any bars?

(LUISA stares at her.)

On your phone?

MARCELA: *Get up.*

GUADALUPE: *I can't walk!*

MARCELA: *You just were!*

GUADALUPE: *I'm too tired.*

MARCELA: *(Turns on GUADALUPE.) Do you know what it's like to be left in the desert? At night, with spiders and rattlesnakes everywhere? And you sit there alone waiting and waiting, hoping that someone will come along. But they don't, and you're all by yourself, you're so small in the middle of these mountains. This desert, it's huge, no one can find you out here, not even God. Your prayers don't work out here, there's no reception.*

(Pause.)

I'm not leaving anyone.

(After a moment, GUADALUPE starts gathering her things and putting them in her backpack.)

ALEJANDRA: It'll be an adventure! Four women, making their way together. Like the Sex and the City!

(Beat. All look at ALEJANDRA.)

MARCELA: (To GUADALUPE.) I'll carry your backpack.

GUADALUPE: (Grabs it quickly.) No, I've got it. You take the water.

MARCELA: (Freezes) Where's our water?

(GUADALUPE and MARCELA look at each other. Lights shift to interview area. LUISA is sitting, being interviewed by the actor who plays MARCELA.)

INTERVIEWER: *Thank you for talking to me. I know you must be very tired.*

(Pause.)

My name is Alma de la Cruz and I'm a researcher. I research issues about the border, and right now I'm doing a project about women and migration. Specifically, I'm theorizing the intersection between women, their social and economic context, and immigration enforcement and I'd like to interview you. Is that all right?

(LUISA smiles and nods.)

Great. Let me start this.

(She takes out a tape recorder, puts it on the table, and presses a button. LUISA stares at the recorder.)

It's so I remember everything. Is that OK?

(LUISA smiles.)

You'll forget it's there, don't worry. So where are you from?

LUISA: *Zinacantán.*

INTERVIEWER: *Chiapas?*

(LUISA nods.)

Do you have family in the U.S.?

(LUISA smiles but doesn't answer.)

Do you know where you're going in the U.S.?

(Nods and smiles.)

Where are you going?

(No answer.)

It's all right. You don't have to tell me if you don't feel comfortable.

(Pause.)

Um...so why are you coming to the U.S.?

LUISA: For the hurricane.

INTERVIEWER: The hurricane?

(LUISA nods.)

What happened?

LUISA: The ground was gone.

INTERVIEWER: *The ground was gone? What do you mean?*

LUISA: *The river took the ground away. We try to put the plants but there's no ground.*

INTERVIEWER: *Oh, the soil's gone! There was lots of erosion.*

(*LUISA nods and smiles.*)

So you couldn't farm anymore.

LUISA: *In my community, everyone does to help the other. We are together, we share, nothing is for only one. My father says, "We are family, we must stay together." We always live that way.*

INTERVIEWER: *So why did you leave?*

(*LUISA doesn't answer.*)

That must have been a long trip by yourself.

(*Nods.*)

Dangerous. Especially for a woman traveling alone.

(*Nods.*)

Many women are assaulted on the way to the U.S.

(*Smiles.*)

Did anything like that happen to you?

(*Smiles and looks away.*)

Were you assaulted?

(*Smiles.*)

Were you raped?

(*Smiles. Long silence.*)

I'm sorry. I know it can be very difficult to talk about.

(*Smiles and shakes her head.*)

It's not difficult?

LUISA: No.

(*Confused silence. Light bulb goes on for INTERVIEWER.*)

INTERVIEWER: *Luisa, do you speak Spanish? Do you understand what I'm saying?*

LUISA: *A little.*

    (Lights shift to four women walking.)

GUADALUPE: *I have to sit down, my ankle hurts.*

                    (She sits.)

Where's the water?

MARCELA: *There's not much left.*

    (The other three sit, LUISA pulls out a jug of water and passes it around, everyone drinks.)

GUADALUPE: *I keep hearing footsteps.*

          (Pause.)

Do you hear them?

MARCELA: *No.*

ALEJANDRA: *No.*

GUADALUPE: *I keep hearing footsteps. Do you think they're tracking us?*

25

MARCELA: *Who, migra? Why would they track us?*

GUADALUPE: *To follow us. To see where we're going.*

MARCELA: *If they knew we were here, they'd grab us. They wouldn't waste time following.*

GUADALUPE: *(Slaps LUISA's hand as she's drinking.) That's enough!*

MARCELA: *It's her water. She's sharing it.*

GUADALUPE: *It's almost gone.*

(Beat.)

ALEJANDRA: *What are they like?*

MARCELA: *Migra?*

ALEJANDRA: *The officers.*

MARCELA: *Most are fine. If you don't run, they're polite. They make you dump your food, give you water, four crackers. One asked us what kind of music we wanted to listen to on the way to the detention center. When he dropped us off, he wished us better luck next time.*

GUADALUPE: *Really?*

ALEJANDRA: *That's so nice!*

MARCELA: *That's most. But some of them are angry. Usually Chicanos. They don't want to think about how close they came to being us.*

ALEJANDRA: *What do they do?*

MARCELA: *They make you lie on the ground and kick you. Even when you're just laying there, not doing anything. They kick you in the stomach, over and over.*

GUADALUPE: *The women too?*

MARCELA: *No, mostly the men. The women they just call ugly whores.*

GUADALUPE: *You'd think they'd remember where they came from. Stop abusing their power.*

MARCELA:(Laughing.) *What power? If they had any power, they wouldn't be out here beating us up.*

ALEJANDRA: *So what's it like there?*

MARCELA: *In the U.S.?*

ALEJANDRA: Yes!

MARCELA: You have to look down a lot. Don't make eye contact. Don't speak Spanish in public. Only the Mexicans shopping with visas speak Spanish in public.

ALEJANDRA: What if someone asks you a question?

MARCELA: Just smile and look away. Then they don't know whether you're illegal or shy. Always have your money out and ready to pay. Be nice to the cashiers and the waiters. Everyone can report you, they have special phone numbers.

GUADALUPE: Like informants?

MARCELA: Yes, except they don't hide it. Get rid of any ID – even if it's real, they'll say it's fake. Don't ride in old beat-up cars with other Mexicans, that's a sure way to get pulled over.

GUADALUPE: What if that's the only ride you have?

MARCELA: Then at least make sure all the lights are working.

GUADALUPE: Why?

MARCELA: That's how they get you — broken taillight, cracked windshield, low tire. Your car has to be perfect. Do an inspection before you get in.

ALEJANDRA: I'll take the bus.

MARCELA: Try to buy a jacket that has a sports team on it. Then find out the name of one of the players. A white one, not brown. Go Romo! Kiss the Jessica!

ALEJANDRA: Who's Jessica?

MARCELA: And don't ride with anyone who's been drinking or taking drugs.

GUADALUPE: What if someone asks you where you're from?

MARCELA: If they're white, you say, "Oh, I'm here from Costa Rica visiting my sister. Your country is so beautiful!" Don't ever say you're Mexican. If you're Mexican, you're illegal.

GUADALUPE: But I'm Guatemalan.

MARCELA: Guatemalans are Mexican.
Salvadorans are Mexicans. If you're illegal,
you're Mexican. If you're Mexican, you're illegal.

GUADALUPE: They don't know much.

MARCELA: Except if you're Cuban.
Then...(Pretends to roll out a carpet in front of
GUADALUPE.) Oh, madam, please welcome to
our country, here is your glass of champagne,
here is your green card. Thank you so much for
opposing that communist monster — would you
like to vote tomorrow?"

GUADALUPE: They get a green card?

MARCELA: The day they arrive.

ALEJANDRA: Well, that's not fair.

   (GUADALUPE and MARCELA look at her.)

GUADALUPE: I've heard they can't even tell the
difference between us and the Indians.

     (Gestures to LUISA.)

They just think we're all brown.

ALEJANDRA: I heard you can make a thousand
pesos a day.

MARCELA: Sometimes. If you're lucky. And your boss is nice.

GUADALUPE: A thousand pesos a day? I could go back in —

(Calculates.)

Two or three years!

MARCELA: You won't.

GUADALUPE: I will. My children are there.

MARCELA: You'll send them money for a while. They'll buy school supplies, new shoes, a Quinceañera dress. And you'll get some things for yourself: a vacuum cleaner, a TV, a nice coat. And two years will turn into three or four, and you'll send for the children. And they'll come and go to school and make friends, and you'll talk to them in Spanish and they'll answer in English. And you'll try to teach them about their country and they'll say, "That shithole! I don't ever want to go back there."

GUADALUPE: My children will never say that.

MARCELA: It's the American Dream. Except Mexican.

GUADALUPE: *You don't know what I'm going to do.*

(Pause.)

How long have you lived in the U.S.?

MARCELA: *Nine years.*

GUADALUPE: *Do you have children?*

MARCELA: *Two daughters in Houston. Sixteen and nineteen.*

(Pause. Starts to get up.)

Let's go...ow!

ALEJANDRA: *What happened?*

MARCELA: *My foot, something in my shoe.*

(She sits down, takes off shoe, feels around inside it.)

GUADALUPE: *Are we going to pass through Arizona? I don't want to go there.*

MARCELA: (Laughs.) Where do you think we are? Ale, there's something on the bottom of my foot, right here, can you get it off?

GUADALUPE: We're in Arizona?

MARCELA: Of course!

GUADALUPE: Well...aren't they supposed to ask for our papers?

MARCELA: Out here?

ALEJANDRA: It won't come off.

MARCELA: What is it?

ALEJANDRA: A blister.

MARCELA: (Stops laughing, looks at ALEJANDRA.) All of it?

(Lights shift. GUADALUPE is in interview area, talking to INTERVIEWER played by ALEJANDRA.)

GUADALUPE: He told me I was a lioness.

INTERVIEWER: What?

GUADALUPE: *We have two young children. And he's older, my husband, about fifty. He can't work anymore because of his knee. I had a good job, I worked at a pharmacy. I liked it, but there wasn't enough money for school uniforms, supplies, the money just kept...going away.*

(Pause.)

And so my husband, he told me I was a lioness. That with lions, it's the mother who goes out and hunts for food. The father stays back with the cubs. She makes a kill, a goat or a gazelle, and then brings it back to the family so they can eat. He told me that I needed to go to the U.S. to make a kill. He told me I was a lioness.

(Pause.)

He really loves me.

(INTERVIEWER suddenly stands up and yells "STOP!" to an unknown person across the stage.)

(Lights shift from interview area to MARCELA frozen in a half squatting position, as though she were about to sit down. ALEJANDRA sheds INTERVIEWER persona and slowly walks towards her. Sound of a rattle.)

MARCELA: Where is it?

ALEJANDRA: Right behind you.

MARCELA: Can it reach me?

ALEJANDRA: Yes.

(Sound of a rattle.)

MARCELA: Is it coiled?

ALEJANDRA: What do you mean?

MARCELA: Is it wrapped in a circle? Or is it stretched out?

ALEJANDRA: It's, uh...it's, um...kind of in a circle. It's kind of wavy and swervy.

MARCELA: (Pause.) What?

ALEJANDRA: Wait – (Pause.) It's moving.

MARCELA: Where?

ALEJANDRA: I'm not sure.

MARCELA: Towards me?

ALEJANDRA: Um...

MARCELA: *Should I move?*

ALEJANDRA: *No, stay still.*

MARCELA: *Shit!*

ALEJANDRA: *(Pause.) It's moving away.*

(Pause.)

Now walk forward and to the left.

(MARCELA does so.)

You're fine.

(MARCELA turns around.)

MARCELA: *Where is it?*

(ALEJANDRA points.)

My god. It's huge.

(Pause.)

That would have been it. That would have been the end of me. I couldn't have walked; I would have died from the poison. You all would have left me here. It would have been the end of me.

ALEJANDRA: You're fine. We wouldn't have left you here.

MARCELA: (Nervous laughter.) "Kind of wavy and swervy"? What is that?

ALEJANDRA: (Laughs.) I don't know. It wasn't straight; it wasn't curled up in a circle. It was...wavy and swervy.

(They giggle.)

MARCELA: You remind me a lot of my daughter.

(Pause.)

So why are you headed north?

ALEJANDRA: Well, you know, it's an adventure! I've lived my whole life in the city; it's time to see something new.

MARCELA: What do you want to do there?

ALEJANDRA: I don't know — shop, look around, see if it's like everyone says! I just got so tired of where I was.

(Pause.)

Every day I'd walk past the same places: same streets, same houses, same barking dogs, same men at food stands. My eyes wanted to see something different, something new.

MARCELA: (Gesturing to the desert.) This must be new.

ALEJANDRA: On my way to school, I had to walk on the edge of this neighborhood. The dump neighborhood, where they take all the garbage every day. Have you seen it? It goes on for miles and miles, off into the horizon. And there's children there, these poor little children living in the dump, picking through garbage, playing in green puddles. They wear filthy t-shirts that say "Oakland Raiders" and their little feet have infected cuts all over them and they dig through hills of trash every day to find something to eat or sell...

(She trails off. Silence.)

MARCELA: No one should ever have to do that.

ALEJANDRA: (Almost ferocious.) Well, then why do they? Why would you make your kids live like that? It's disgusting. In the U.S no one lives in garbage dumps. I don't ever want to be in a place where I see that again.

MARCELA: (*Wryly.*) Actually you're exactly like my daughter.

(*Pause.*)

ALEJANDRA: How's your blister?

MARCELA: Getting bigger.

ALEJANDRA: Does it hurt?

MARCELA: Not yet. It will soon.

ALEJANDRA: Then what?

MARCELA: I might not be able to walk.

(*Silence.*)

ALEJANDRA: Did you get left out here once?

(*MARCELA nods. Silence.*)

What happened?

MARCELA: I came with two of my nephews, we joined a bigger group. On the second day, I started falling behind. They were nice. Stayed back to help, kept encouraging me. But I could see the guide talking to them. They'd look over at

39

me, talk, look back. They didn't walk with me anymore, kept going way ahead.

(Pause.)

Then when I was trying to catch up, I fell down a bank. I started yelling and they came back. The guide looked at my knee and shook his head. It was getting dark. They left me some water.

ALEJANDRA: They left you there? How they could do that?

MARCELA: It's the choices we make. People say they'll be loyal but it all comes down to that moment. It's like Jesus and Peter. Jesus tells the disciples they're all going to leave him. And Peter denies it. He swears, "Lord, even if I have to die with you, I'll never betray you." Jesus tells him that he'll deny him three times before the cockcrows twice. And he does.

ALEJANDRA: But you know you're leaving someone to die! A human being, your own family!

MARCELA: There's a moment when they have to decide. They weigh it — you can see them thinking about their kids, a new house, the money. They look at you and wonder, how many more years would she actually live anyway? Then they decide: the life of an old woman I don't even really know or my family and my American dream?

(Silence.)

ALEJANDRA: *I wouldn't leave you.*
MARCELA: *Don't say that. Don't say that unless you know for sure.*

ALEJANDRA: *I do.*

MARCELA: *I wouldn't leave you either.*

ALEJANDRA: *(Pause.) So what happened?*

MARCELA: *I got mad. I said I wasn't going to die out here. So I dragged myself to a road. Three days.*

ALEJANDRA: *You crawled to a road?*

MARCELA: *Not crawled, dragged. I had two sticks and just kept pulling myself forward on the ground.*

ALEJANDRA: *Wow...*

MARCELA: *You think walking is bad, try that. Hands bloody, thorns everywhere, my bad knee dragging behind.*

ALEJANDRA: *Kind of wavy and swervy?*

(MARCELA looks at ALEJANDRA for a moment, then bursts out laughing. She stands up and begins to walk again.)

(ALEJANDRA starts to follow her and then stops. She goes back to where the snake was, stares at it. She picks up a small rock and throws it in the vicinity of the snake. Sound of the rattle. She stares at it.)

(Lights shift to interview area, with LUISA and INTERVIEWER played by MARCELA.)

INTERVIEWER: Were you scared?

LUISA: Scared?

INTERVIEWER: Were you afraid? That something might happen to you?

LUISA: No.

INTERVIEWER: Not at all?

LUISA: No.

INTERVIEWER: You understand what I'm saying?

LUISA: Yes.

INTERVIEWER: *But you weren't scared?*

LUISA: *No.*

INTERVIEWER: *Many people die in the desert.*

(*Pause.*)

You must have seen some of the clothes. The backpacks and water bottles. The shoes.

(*Pause.*)

Maybe you even saw the bodies.

LUISA: *I smell them.*

INTERVIEWER: *You smelled them?*

LUISA: *I would walk...and then the hot and cold would change. If it was hot, it would go cold. If it was cold, it would go hot. And then I smell them.*

INTERVIEWER: *And you weren't scared?*

(*Silence.*)

Do you understand what I'm asking?

LUISA: Near my community there's cows.

INTERVIEWER: (Confused pause.) Yes?

LUISA: A rich man owns the cows and he feeds them corn.

INTERVIEWER: OK.

LUISA: Sometimes when people from my community are very hungry, they go to the cow field.

INTERVIEWER: Yes?

LUISA: (Overlapping INTERVIEWER's line.) And pick pieces of corn out of the cow shit.

(INTERVIEWER grows pale.)

They wash it first.

(Pause, looks at INTERVIEWER.)

I wasn't scared.

(Silence. Lights shift to ALEJANDRA and GUADALUPE staggering slightly until they come to rest on the ground. MARCELA and LUISA follow behind.)

MARCELA: *We're out of water?*

GUADALUPE: *Yes.*

ALEJANDRA: *(Shivers.) It's getting cold.*

MARCELA: *I think I recognize that mountain.*

(Pause.)

At least it's not summer. We never would have made it in summer.

GUADALUPE: *I still hear footsteps. How much farther?*

MARCELA: *Probably another day to Tucson.*

GUADALUPE: *Another day! You said we were almost there!*

MARCELA: *That's what guides say. And now I'm the guide so I have to say it too.*

(Imitating.)

"Come on, come on, go faster, go faster, it's only on the other side of this mountain, the ride is waiting for us!"

*(All make an attempt to laugh except
GUADALUPE.)*

*GUADALUPE: Will it be funny when I'm lying
in a ditch and can't keep walking?*

MARCELA: You can make it.

GUADALUPE: No, I can't.

(Silence.)

*ALEJANDRA: (Suddenly, to all.) What do you
think about when you're walking?*

*MARCELA: I think, this must be how Moses and
the Israelites felt, after they left Egypt. For forty
years, wandering the desert — can you imagine?
We've only been two days.*

*GUADALUPE: At least they had their kids
along.*

*MARCELA: There must be something about the
desert. Some reason God keeps bringing His
people out here.*

(To ALEJANDRA.)

What do you think about?

ALEJANDRA: I think about the dress that I'm going to buy my sister for her Quinceañera. I think about all the styles, then I think about all the colors, then I imagine each style in each color, then I think about shoes with each style in each color...

MARCELA: Don't do green.

GUADALUPE: That's why you're going? To buy your sister a dress?

ALEJANDRA: And to see the U.S. I always wanted to see what it was like.

GUADALUPE: (Under her breath.) Chilanga.

ALEJANDRA: (To GUADALUPE.) What do you think about?

GUADALUPE: I think about my family. My children. I say —

(Demonstrates.)

"This step is for Lourdes. This step is for Mario. This step is for my mother. This step is for my father. This step is for me. So I'll be happy." Then I start all over. And after a while, my mind goes white.

MARCELA: Your husband?

GUADALUPE: Of course. "This step is for my husband." Of course.

(Beat.)

ALEJANDRA: (To LUISA.) What do you think about?

LUISA: What?

ALEJANDRA: When you're walking. What do you think about?

LUISA: Nothing.

ALEJANDRA: You don't think about anything? You have to think about something. Your family. Your feet.

LUISA: (Short pause.) I think about stories.

ALEJANDRA: What stories?

LUISA: Stories that women tell. About the old times.

GUADALUPE: Indian stories.

LUISA: *Yes. I try to remember them. Remember how they go.*

MARCELA: *Tell us one.*

LUISA: *(Slight panicked.) Now?*

MARCELA: *Yes. We need to rest. Tell us an Indian story.*

LUISA: *I can't speak so good.*

ALEJANDRA: *We'll help you.*

(Long pause.)

LUISA: *My grandmother tell this story about a woman.*

(Pause. Puts her hand half way over her mouth.)

She was married to a man and they are in love. So in love. They always want to be together, not —

(Looks at ALEJANDRA.)

ALEJANDRA: *Separated?*

LUISA: *Separated. They want to be together, not separate.*

(Pause.)

But they were very poor. And they don't have enough to eat. So sometimes they have to —

ALEJANDRA: Take your hand down.

LUISA: What?

ALEJANDRA: Take your hand down.

(Pause. ALEJANDRA pulls LUISA's hand away from her mouth. LUISA looks frightened.)

Keep going.

LUISA: Sometimes they have no food for days. Every night they can hardly sleep because their stomachs are barking.

(She covers her mouth with her hand again. ALEJANDRA again pulls it down.)

LUISA: One morning, the husband sees that the wife's teeth are all black. He thinks, what would give her the black teeth, are they rotting? But when she drinks water, the black washes off.

(ALEJANDRA pulls her hand away and holds it.)

LUISA: *Every morning the wife wakes up with black teeth. The husband asks her why, but she says, "I don't know."*

(We hear music and the lights begin to change. During the following section, LUISA loses her self-consciousness and begins to act out the story using movement. Perhaps the other women also do movement; perhaps there is multimedia or props, anything to create an alternate world in which the story is told.)

LUISA: *That night the husband wakes up and hears something moving across the floor. He looks over to his wife and sees that she has no head. It's only her body and her neck lying beside him.*

The husband hears the sound again. He sits up and sees that the sound is his wife's head. Her head is rolling across the floor. It rolls toward the fire, opens its mouth and starts to eat the ashes. It eats for a long time. Then it rolls up the side of the bed and puts itself back on the wife's body.

The next day the husband leaves early and goes to every part of the village to find work. He works very hard and gets some money to buy tortillas and beans and a little piece of chicken.

He takes it to his wife and they are very happy, happy to be eating.

The husband works hard every day and brings home food for them each night. After they eat, he falls into bed and sleeps right away.

One day the husband wakes up very early to leave for a job. As he gets out of bed, he hears the same noise. He looks to the fire and once again sees his wife's head eating ashes. He watches as it eats and eats the ashes, more ashes than before. Finally the man cannot suffer it anymore and calls out to the head, "Why do you betray me?"

The head hears him because it still has ears. Then it starts to roll. It rolls away from him across the floor. The door opens and the head leaves the house, rolling through the front yard and past the neighbors' house and down the road. The man waits and waits but the head never comes back.

(Music ends, lights return to normal.)

GUADALUPE: *Indian stories.*

ALEJANDRA: *Wow.*

MARCELA: *Where did you get that?*

LUISA: *(To MARCELA.) From you.*

MARCELA: *What?*

LUISA: *It's your story.*

(Long pause.)

MARCELA: *What do you mean?*

GUADALUPE: *Don't talk to her like that, it's disrespectful.*
MARCELA: *I'm the wife with black teeth?*

GUADALUPE: *Those stories are crazy, nothing but witchcraft and superstition, they get people all worked up.*

ALEJANDRA: *They're amazing.*

GUADALUPE: *You apologize to her right now.*

MARCELA: *(To GUADALUPE.) Oh, don't take it so seriously; it's just a story. I kind of like the idea of my head rolling around.*

(Thinks for a moment, laughs.)

And I did leave him.

(Stands up and starts walking briskly.)

The moon's out. Let's get going.

ALEJANDRA: Marcela?

MARCELA: What?

ALEJANDRA: That's where we came from. We want to go the other way, right?

MARCELA: (Surprised.) Oh! Right.

GUADALUPE: You know where we're going?

MARCELA: Oh sure, I just got confused for a second.

(She strides off confidently, the other three look at each other and reluctantly follow her. Lights down.)

(Lights rise on ALEJANDRA, walking and looking haggard, carrying her backpack. She takes a few steps and plops on the ground. Breathes heavy. After a few seconds, she starts singing a Madonna song.)

ALEJANDRA: "Faster than the speeding light she's flying Trying to remember where it all began...

(Forgets the words momentarily.)

Da da da da a little piece of heaven
Waiting for the time when Earth shall be as one

And I feel like I just got home
And I feel

Quicker than a ray of light
Quicker than a ray of light..."

(Runs out of breath. LUISA approaches her,
takes her backpack, stands and waits.)

ALEJANDRA: Oh, thank you, Luisa. Thank you
so much. When we get there, I'm definitely
gonna friend you on Facebook.

(Struggles to rise, becomes fascinated by her
arms.)

Look at all my scratches. These stupid trees are
angry at me. They keep reaching out to grab me,
trying to hold me back.

(She moves her arms fluidly, staring at them, like
a sacred dance.)

It's OK, Luisa, you can go ahead.

LUISA: You need to keep walking.

ALEJANDRA: I'll catch up. I'm just going to explain to these dumb trees why they should let me pass.

LUISA: We are family, we must stay together.

(LUISA helps ALEJANDRA stand up; ALEJANDRA starts walking and singing again.)

(Interview area, GUADALUPE being interviewed by actor who plays ALEJANDRA.)

GUADALUPE: When we started, they said it would be a day's walk. They said it would be fine, take some water and you'll be there in no time. They said it's just like a long walk down the beach.

(Starts to cry.)

She was a beautiful spirit.

INTERVIEWER: You believed them?

GUADALUPE: What?

INTERVIEWER: When they said it was a day's walk. A stroll down the beach.

GUADALUPE: Yes.

INTERVIEWER: (Makes notes.) OK.

GUADALUPE: (Pause.) What are you writing?

INTERVIEWER: Nothing.

GUADALUPE: That's what they told me. That it would be easy.

INTERVIEWER: The guides told you that?

GUADALUPE: Yes.

(Pause.)

I'm not stupid. Don't write that I'm stupid.

INTERVIEWER: I'm not writing that you're stupid.

GUADALUPE: You're thinking it.

INTERVIEWER: No, I'm not.

GUADALUPE: You'll think it now and write it later.

INTERVIEWER: (Sighs.) Ma'am, I'm not saying you're stupid. I just get frustrated. I'm a public defender — I talk to hundreds of people charged with illegal entry and I don't get it. It's the desert. It's three days. It's 118 degrees. Of course it's not going to be easy. Why would you believe him?

GUADALUPE: I walked for three days with no food and no water! My shoes were soaked red from the —

INTERVIEWER: I know, I know you've been through a terrible ordeal and left your family behind and sacrificed everything and now the person from your group is dead. But I'm tired of this. I'm tired of seeing people die because they didn't use a little common sense.

GUADALUPE: (Crying.) I was out there for four days with a broken ankle and no food or water —

INTERVIEWER: And here, they're going to say that it was your choice. That you took the risk and knew what could happen. That you have no one to blame but yourself. That's what they're going to say.

(Sigh.)

I mean, seriously, it's the desert. It's 118 degrees. Figure it out.

(Lights shift to MARCELA walking. Suddenly she stops and gasps.)

MARCELA: *Water.*

ALEJANDRA: *What?*

MARCELA: *Water.*

GUADALUPE: *Where? Where do you see it?*

MARCELA: *No, my shoe. My sock is all wet.*

(MARCELA sits down, takes off her shoe. ALEJANDRA looks at it, touches it, MARCELA cries out in pain.)

ALEJANDRA: *It burst.*

MARCELA: *(Half laughing, half crying.) Of course it did, of course it did. The one place on my body where I don't want water.*

(Looks up at the sky.)

Laughing yet?

ALEJANDRA: *You should let it dry out.*

GUADALUPE: *Then what?*

ALEJANDRA: Then we'll figure out what to do.
GUADALUPE: She can't keep walking.

ALEJANDRA: We'll figure it out.

(Sits down, weary. Pause.)

I need another story. Luisa, tell us another one of your stories.

LUISA: (Surprised.) You want to hear a story? One of mine?

ALEJANDRA: Yes. Please.

LUISA: What kind?

ALEJANDRA: Anything. My story. The first one was Marcela's, now tell me my story.

LUISA: Your story?

ALEJANDRA: Is there a story about me?

GUADALUPE: They're bad for you — all that Indian witchcraft and nonsense. No more stories. How much farther is it?

MARCELA: We're almost there.

GUADALUPE: *What does that mean — another hour, another day? Another two days?*

MARCELA: *Not that long.*

GUADALUPE: *Then how long?*

(No answer.)

If you'd let me stay there like I wanted, I'd be home by now. Do you even know where we are?

(MARCELA looks away, doesn't answer. Awkward silence.)

LUISA: *(Defiantly.) A young girl lived in a small village with her family...*

(GUADALUPE shoots LUISA a look of disgust and walks away, not listening.)

The village was very poor but she was beautiful and always happy. Her friends asked why she was never sad, but she laughed and said there was nothing to be sad about. But her friends didn't believe this, they thought she had a mystery, something that always made her happy, a...

(LUISA struggles to think of the word.)

ALEJANDRA: *A boyfriend?*

LUISA: *No, a mystery, a...*

 (Frustrated, trying to come up with the word,
   says something in Tzotzil.)

GUADALUPE: *Secret.*

  (All look at GUADALUPE.)

LUISA: *A secret! They thought she had a secret.
Every night she would go up on a hill by herself
to pray. So one day they followed her.*

 *(Lights change, music begins, go into alternate
     world.)*

LUISA: *When she came to the top, the girl went
to a hollow tree and took out four black candles.
She starts to sing and puts the candles all around
her and lights them. Then she stands in the
middle of the candles and says, "Lay down, skin.
Lay down, skin. Lay down," and the skin falls off
her body. It starts at the head and slides down
until it's lying around her feet like dirty clothes
and she's standing there in nothing but her clean
white bones. Then she rises up and starts to fly.
The friends see her flying above the village,
looking down on all the neighbors and family
and then she disappears.*

The friends wait. After a while, the girl's bones fly back to the hill, and land in the middle of the candles. The bones cry out, "Rise up, skin. Rise up, skin. Rise up." And the skin comes back up to cover her bones until she looks like she always does. Then she blows out the candles, puts them back in the tree, and goes down to the village.

One of the friends goes to talk to an old woman in the village. The next night the old woman takes some salt and limes and climbs the hill with the girl's friends. They see the beautiful girl leave her skin and begin to fly above the village, looking down on all the poor people. As soon as she's gone, the old woman takes out the salt and sprinkles it on top of the skin and then squeezes the limes on it.

When the bones of the beautiful girl return, they fly to where her skin sits and say, "Rise up, skin. Rise up, skin. Rise up." But the skin doesn't rise. The girl looks confused. She says it again, "Rise up, skin. Rise up, skin. Rise up, skin," but nothing happens. Suddenly, the beautiful girl sees her friends and the old woman standing there. She knows what happened, she knows they have done this and she starts to cry. Then she flies away, leaving her skin there and the candles burning, she flies away in her clean white bones and never returns.

(Silence.)

ALEJANDRA: *Wow, that is me! I used to go up on this old hill and sing all the time.*

MARCELA: *What does it mean?*

ALEJANDRA: *I don't know, but I like it! I like that I'm beautiful and I can fly. And that the old woman made my skin into a margarita.*

GUADALUPE: *Indian stories. There's always magic, always people flying, always some kind of witchcraft.*

(Starts gathering things.)

You think your people have special powers, that you can cast spells or tip the world? You're still here with us, still lost in the desert. Why don't you fly up in the wind and see where Tucson is, why don't you turn that cactus into water, why don't you use those magic Indian powers to actually do us some good?

MARCELA: *Lupe —*

LUISA: *We don't have powers. We just listen more.*

(GUADALUPE stalks off.)

ALEJANDRA: (To MARCELA.) I'll get her.

(MARCELA puts her head in her hands. LUISA approaches her and starts to examine her feet. Lights down.)
(Interview area. MARCELA sits with INTERVIEWER, played by GUADALUPE.)

MARCELA: I told them, look girls, you ever see me in trouble, getting questioned, asked for papers, you don't know me. You go home and you wait for me to call. So one day I went to pick up the older one at the bus station. I'm waiting for the bus and I see the green car and the green uniforms pull up. They come in and look around, asking people questions. I sit still, I look at the ground, but the green comes over to me, they ask me questions, they want to see my papers. Right then, the bus gets in. My daughter gets off. She walks right past me. She was so good. Did it exactly the way I told her. Walks right past me.

(Pause.)

Didn't even look at me. Exactly the way I told her.

(Pause. From other area, we hear ALEJANDRA's voice.)

ALEJANDRA: It's a bike!

(Lights shift to ALEJANDRA peering across the desert.)

MARCELA: What?

ALEJANDRA: A bike! Up against that tree!

GUADALUPE: A bike? Your eyes are playing tricks on you.

MARCELA: Why would there be a bike? You can't use it out here, it's too rough.

ALEJANDRA: Don't you see it? Right over there!

GUADALUPE: Ale, why would someone ride a bike across the desert?

MARCELA: And if they got this far on it, why would they leave it?

ALEJANDRA: No, it's there!

(ALEJANDRA runs off.)

MARCELA: Alejandra, don't, it's nothing!

(Quietly.)

She needs water.

GUADALUPE: We all do. How much farther?

MARCELA: Lupe, I don't know. I don't know how much farther, all right?

GUADALUPE: What are we going to do?

MARCELA: There's a highway that we'll cross eventually. If we keep going this way —

ALEJANDRA: Hey look!

(ALEJANDRA rides in on a bike, circles around the women, perhaps ringing the bell.)

MARCELA: (Looks at GUADALUPE.) It's a bike.

ALEJANDRA: It's in pretty good shape. A little rust. I wonder how long it's been out here.

GUADALUPE: What are you going to do with it?

ALEJANDRA: I'm going to ride it for a while. Do you think it belongs to anyone?

MARCELA: (Snorts.) I'm sure they don't care now.

ALEJANDRA: Maybe I can go find some water.

MARCELA: Don't go off on your own.

GUADALUPE: You'll get lost and never find your way back.

ALEJANDRA: I'll just go a little way. Stay right here.

MARCELA: Alejandra!

(ALEJANDRA rides off.)

GUADALUPE: (Sits down.) This is ridiculous. I don't want to be here. I don't want to be in the middle of this godforsaken place. I want to be home with my children.

MARCELA: (Sits down with GUADALUPE.) Me too.

(Pause.)
How many do you have?

GUADALUPE: Two. Mario and Lourdes.

(Starts to cry, everything comes out in a rush.)

Do you know what I really think about when I walk? I think about giving them a bath. Our house is so cold. But for their baths I heat water on the stove and all the windows in the kitchen fog over. It gets so warm and cozy. And I pour the water in their orange plastic tub and they get naked and run around the kitchen screeching and laughing because the water's too hot. But then they get in — one foot, two feet, sit down, pour a cup of water over their heads. And we take things from the kitchen — anything that floats — and pretend that the plastic fork is attacking the cup and the ice cube tray has come to rescue it. Then when the water's starting to get cold, that's the best part.

(Pause.)

I get two towels, the biggest, softest towels we have, and I tell them to stand up. And when their little bodies are naked and dripping and shivering, I swoop in with the towel and wrap it around them and I pick them up and hold them as tight as I can. And I squeeze and squeeze and smell their clean hair and soft skin and they snuggle up to me and I want to stay like that forever. There's no better feeling in the world than holding your children after a bath. That's what I think about when I'm walking.

(Suddenly erupts.)

WHY DO I KEEP HEARING FOOTSTEPS?!

ALEJANDRA: Hey!

(ALEJANDRA rides up.)

ALEJANDRA: There's a flag over there! And it's got a whole bunch of water underneath it!

(She holds up a full gallon jug. MARCELA immediately gets to her feet and follows, leaving GUADALUPE to sit by herself.)

(Lights shift to interview area. ALEJANDRA sits at the table alone. The INTERVIEWER, played by the actor who portrays LUISA, enters. INTERVIEWER sits, says nothing, they look at one another. Silence. Actors freeze.)

(GUADALUPE comes to interview area, switches places with LUISA. ALEJANDRA becomes INTERVIEWER.)

INTERVIEWER: You might get time served. But probably more like one to three.

GUADALUPE: Days?

INTERVIEWER: Months.

GUADALUPE: But I didn't do anything! I'm just here to work. They're the ones who did it. They're the ones who lied to us and robbed us and said it'd only take a day. I just came here to work, I didn't do anything wrong.

INTERVIEWER: You had fifteen pounds of cocaine.

GUADALUPE: It was cheaper that way! Two thousand if you didn't carry, twelve hundred if you did. I didn't have two thousand! What was I supposed to do? What would you have done?

(Silence.)

So after I get out, I'll be able to work?

INTERVIEWER: No. You'll be deported.

GUADALUPE: I can't get a work permit for a year or two?

INTERVIEWER: No.

GUADALUPE: A few months?

INTERVIEWER: No.

GUADALUPE: *(Starts crying.) This country is supposed to be about freedom. Freedom and democracy. Where's my rights? Where's my freedom? Look. Look at this.*

(Pulls out several pictures, shows them to interviewer.)

These are my children. All of them. Two — five children. They need to eat. I need to feed them. Why won't you let me feed them? If I can't feed them, what am I good for? I might as well kill myself. I might as well kill myself right now.
INTERVIEWER: *Look, the fact is you broke the law. You entered the country illegally. That's against the law. You brought drugs into the country. That's against the law. I understand why you did it but you broke the law. And there's nothing that gives you the right to stay here and work. So I want to help you but there's nothing I can do.*

GUADALUPE: *(Stares coldly at INTERVIEWER.) Thank you for your help.*

(Lights fade and rise on women walking. MARCELA is in good spirits, leading the way.)

MARCELA: *Now we're fine. We've got all the water we need, I know where we're at, it's only a few more miles. Are you ready to see the famous Gringoland?*

GUADALUPE: *How will we get anywhere? We missed our ride.*

MARCELA: *I have a cousin in Phoenix. We'll find a phone along the highway and call him. He can take us in for the night and then to the bus station tomorrow.*

ALEJANDRA: *(Excited.) Where should I go? I was thinking New York but I heard it's far.*

MARCELA: *Chicago's closer. It's got everything New York does but closer.*

ALEJANDRA: *(To GUADALUPE.) Where are you going?*

GUADALUPE: *Washington.*

MARCELA: *Which one?*

GUADALUPE: *What do you mean?*

MARCELA: *There's two.*

GUADALUPE: *There's two?*

MARCELA: One in the east where the president lives and one in the west by Canada.

ALEJANDRA: They have two of everything!

MARCELA: Which one are you going to?

GUADALUPE: I don't know. I guess I'll just pick one. And if I get it wrong, I'll go to the other one.
ALEJANDRA: (To LUISA.) Where are you going?

> *(LUISA*
> *shrugs.)*

You can come with me to Chicago.

GUADALUPE: (To MARCELA.) Are your daughters still in Houston?

MARCELA: Yes. A day in Phoenix, two days on the bus and I'll see them!

ALEJANDRA: How long has it been?

MARCELA: Two and a half months. Too long.

ALEJANDRA: But, it's almost over. Oh!

(ALEJANDRA stops in her tracks. Other women stop as well.)

We forgot something.

MARCELA: *What?*

ALEJANDRA: *We can't go on without it.*

> *(Points to
> LUISA.)*

We have to hear Guadalupe's story.

> *(GUADALUPE
> starts walking again.)*

MARCELA: *No, we don't.*

ALEJANDRA: *No, we can't finish our walk until
we hear the last one!*

GUADALUPE: *I don't have a story.*

MARCELA: *Alejandra, let —*

GUADALUPE: *(Turns to LUISA.) You know
what? Fine. Tell me a good Indian story. It's
getting dark; we can rest till the moon rises. Go
ahead; tell me a good Indian story.*

> *(They all look at LUISA. As she starts talking,
> lights change, music and movement begin.)*

LUISA: There was a man who was a hunter. And most days, he would tell his wife, "I am leaving to hunt deer." But he didn't hunt deer. He would go to the house of his lover and then buy deer on the path home.

One day the wife was in the village and a neighbor said to her, "Tell your husband that I have some good deer meat to buy." She said, "Why would my husband buy your meat? He hunts it himself every day." But when the neighbor walked away, she starts to think. And then she knows what is happening.

The next day when her husband comes home, she asks him how was the hunting. He says, "Good, don't you see that I brought you this meat?" So she cooked the meat and then after the meal she gives him wine, lots and lots of wine until the husband becomes drunk and falls asleep in the bed.

Once he is drunk, the wife pulls off the blankets and opens his pants. She takes his penis and bends it farther and farther until it snaps off. Then she brings a carrot and her sewing things to the bed. In place of the penis, his wife sews on a carrot where the penis used to be. She takes a long time and makes nice stitches so the carrot fits right. Then she goes to sleep.

The next morning, the husband wakes up and says to himself, "That was a good night." He eats breakfast and tells the wife, "I am leaving to hunt deer." The wife says, "Good, come home tonight because I am making tamales."

But the husband does not go to hunt; he goes to the house of his lover. His lover sends the children away, but when they start, she cries out. It hurts because the wife did not trim the carrot; it is still long and pointy with the little string hanging off the end. She tells him, "I can't be made love to by a carrot!" and sends him away.

The husband feels hurt as he walks home. But he remembers that his wife is making tamales and he wonders if she has more wine for him. When he gets home, she brings him a plate of tamales and he starts eating very fast. Suddenly, he is thirsty and needs water. He drinks one glass of water and then more and more.

The husband asks the wife, "What did you put in those tamales that makes me so thirsty?" She says, "I filled them with your penis." Then the husband opens his pants and realizes that it's a carrot between his legs and he's been eating his penis all along. But he cannot stop from drinking water and he drinks and drinks until he becomes very ill. He goes to bed and dies three days later and they bury him by the river.

(Silence.)

MARCELA: Oh my god.

ALEJANDRA: That's amazing!

MARCELAL: Where did that —

GUADALUPE: (To LUISA.) Why is that my story?

(GUADALUPE gets up, slowly starts walking towards LUISA.)

Why is that my story?

MARCELA: Guadalupe, just let it —

GUADALUPE: No, I want you to tell me. Why is that my story, you little whore?

MARCELA: Lupe!

ALEJANDRA: Don't be upset, it's funny!

GUADALUPE: It's not funny. And it's none of your business. None of your business what happens in my family. I told you to stop telling those stories so shut up!

MARCELA: *Lupe, that's enough.*

GUADALUPE: *You don't know my life. I know yours but you don't know mine. I know the things you did to get here — dirty things. Stop pretending like you're one of us and go back to the mountains!*

(Pacing.)

He just goes to see the children. He doesn't love her. And he doesn't go every day, only Saturdays. Sometimes Fridays and Sundays. He's...

(Starts to cry.)

There wasn't enough money for all of us. For notebooks and uniforms and soap and chicken and...But why did I have to go? Why couldn't it be her? Why did he make me come? Now I'm wandering around in the middle of this stupid desert and she...

(Sobs.)

She's holding them after their bath.

(MARCELA and ALEJANDRA go to console GUADALUPE.)

MARCELA: *He trusted you. He knew you had the best chance of making it. It doesn't mean he doesn't love you, it just means he trusted you more.*

ALEJANDRA: *He wouldn't risk his family by sending someone who wouldn't make it.*

MARCELA: *Exactly.*

GUADALUPE: *And she's stupid. She never would have made it.*

MARCELA: *See? He's doing what's best for his children; it doesn't mean he doesn't love you.*

ALEJANDRA: *I think it means he loves you more.*

GUADALUPE: *(Thinking.) You're right. He loves me more because I'm the one who could make it. I'm the one who can provide. He has to be nice to her because of the children. But he doesn't trust her. He doesn't love her.*

LUISA: *Then why does he go there every weekend?*

(All look at LUISA with shock, GUADALUPE with a look of pure hatred. She strides over and raises her hand, LUISA doesn't flinch. GUADALUPE freezes.)

GUADALUPE: *What's that?*

MARCELA: *What?*

GUADALUPE: *(Whisper) Do you hear it?*

MARCELA: *What?*

GUADALUPE: *That sound. The breathing.*

> *(Silence.)*

MARCELA: *I don't hear it.*

GUADALUPE: *Slow, husky. In and out. Like this.*

> *(She demonstrates. Pause.)*

There! Do you hear it?

MARCELA: *No.*

ALEJANDRA: *I do.*

> *(Silence.)*

ALEJANDRA: *Do we run?*

GUADALUPE: *Which way? They're everywhere!*

MARCELA: *Don't run. If you run, they beat you.*

> *(Clears throat.*
> *In a loud voice.)*

Hello!

> *(No answer.)*

We're here! We're not going to run.

> *(Silence.)*

You can come get us.

> *(Silence.)*

Hello?

> *(Silence. The small sound of a cowbell.*
> *MARCELA begins laughing.)*

GUADALUPE: *What is it?*

LUISA: *It's cows.*

GUADALUPE: *Are you sure?*

LUISA: *Yes.*

ALEJANDRA: *Oh my god.*
GUADALUPE: *You're sure it's cows?*

LUISA: *Yes.*

MARCELA: *(Still laughing uncontrollably.) No, no, it's not just cows, it's Migra Cows! They don't have enough Border Patrol so they're deputizing the cows. Spreading them out along the border. "Can I see your documents, ma'am? MOO!"*

ALEJANDRA: *(Wandering off.) Where are they?*

(LUISA starts to giggle.)

GUADALUPE: *(To LUISA.) Don't laugh at her, we almost died!*

MARCELA: *From what? Death by milking?*

(LUISA laughs. MARCELA approaches one of the cows, holding out her hand.)

Please sir, here's my visa, I know it's expired but I just need to come to your wonderful country and scrub your floors so my little one won't starve. What's that? Only if I give you some hay in return? Oh sir, please have mercy, I don't have any hay on me. What? "Get out now, pinche Mexicana?"

(Turns to LUISA and MARCELA in amazement.)

Even their cows hate us.

> *(GUADALUPE finally bursts out laughing, followed by LUISA and MARCELA. After a moment, LUISA looks up. We hear a thud, followed by a scream.)*

LUISA: Alejandra?

> *(No answer.)*

ALEJANDRA?

MARCELA: Where are you?

ALEJANDRA: Over here. I fell.

> *(They search and eventually find her.)*

MARCELA: What happened?
ALEJANDRA: (Panicking.) I fell off the bank. It's OK, I'm OK...

> *(MARCELA leans down to inspect.)*

MARCELA: Oh my god. No, it's not OK, Ale, I can see the bone.

GUADALUPE: Oh god...

LUISA: Can you walk?

ALEJANDRA: I think I can.

(She tries and cries out in pain, falls.)

OK, wait, let me try again.

(She barely moves, grimaces in pain.)

Give me a little time, I can make it.

(GUADALUPE looks at MARCELA. MARCELA straightens up, takes a deep breath.)

MARCELA: You're going to be fine.

(MARCELA starts to gather her things. She takes some food out of her bag and sets it next to ALEJANDRA.)

ALEJANDRA: Maybe I can rest overnight and it'll hurt less in the morning. We can probably make a cast out of some sticks or something...

(GUADALUPE starts gathering things.)

What's going on?

(MARCELA comes back, touches ALEJANDRA's hair.)

MARCELA: You're strong and you're going to be fine. Remember how to fly.

(MARCELA and GUADALUPE begin walking away.)

ALEJANDRA: What are you...? You're leaving me? You're leaving me here?

(Pause.)
I wasn't going to leave you. I told you I'd never leave you. Don't, please don't. I don't want to die here.

(Pause.)
This is what you hated. You hated them for leaving you behind. For the American dream, the Mexican dream, the famous dream where you leave everyone behind. Look at you, with your black teeth, aren't you proud of yourself? Aren't your daughters proud of you?

(MARCELA stops for a moment, then starts walking again.)

*I can't believe this. I expected this from everyone
else but you. You're really leaving me here?
YOU'RE LEAVING ME HERE?*

   (ALEJANDRA sobs. LUISA touches her hair.)

*ALEJANDRA: You should go too. Don't stay.
Please go.*

LUISA: We'll be OK.

*ALEJANDRA: No we won't. Look at my leg. I
can't walk. The bone, you can feel the bone.*

                              *(Slightly
maniacal laugh.)*

I am a skeleton.

LUISA: We'll make it.

*ALEJANDRA: No we won't. We're going to die
here.*

LUISA: We're not going to die. Does it hurt?

ALEJANDRA: Yes.

LUISA: Try to lean on me.

(LUISA helps ALEJANDRA up, puts ALEJANDRA's arm around LUISA's shoulder and tries to help her walk. After a few steps, ALEJANDRA grimaces.)

ALEJANDRA: Ow. Ow, ow, OW! Stop, please stop!

> *(LUISA stops.)*

ALEJANDRA: *(Half laughing, half crying.)* Where's my bike? I need my bike!

(Shift to MARCELA and GUADALUPE walking in silence.)

GUADALUPE: You didn't have a choice.

> *(MARCELA doesn't respond.)*

She couldn't make it. We all would have died.

> *(Silence.)*

She doesn't have children. You do. Your daughters need you.

MARCELA: I just…

(Pause, stops walking.)

I didn't think it would be so easy.

(Long silence. They start walking again.)

GUADALUPE: (Thinking to herself.) I like the carrot. That was good.

(Shift back to ALEJANDRA and LUISA.)

ALEJANDRA: We'll have to find Border Patrol. I can't make it.

(Pause.)

Maybe you can walk to a road and tell them where I am. We'll both get deported but you can try again.

LUISA: Maybe.

ALEJANDRA: (Pause) No. You can still catch up with them. You need to go on.

LUISA: No.

ALEJANDRA: *They're not that far ahead, start going that way and you'll catch up, they don't walk very fast.*

LUISA: *They don't make it.*

ALEJANDRA: *Luisa, please, please, go. It's OK, I understand, I want you to.*

LUISA: *No.*

ALEJANDRA: *Will you stop saying no? I'm not asking, I'm telling you to do this. Turn around right now and start walking.*

(Silence.)

LUISA: *There was once a girl who lived with her family in the mountains. They had a little piece of land where they grew corn. They didn't have much money, but they were happy together.*

ALEJANDRA: *What?*

(The lights begin to dim, transition into the fantasy world, music starts.)

LUISA: *One day her little brother got sick. He started to vomit snakes, pale white snakes that were alive and twisting. As soon as they came out his mouth, the snakes would leave, slithering out the door, going north. The boy was weak; they didn't know how much longer he would live. But the girl was brave. She said, "I'm going to follow these snakes back to where they come from and tell them to stop making my brother sick."*

The family begged her not to go but she knew that if she didn't her brother would die. She walked for three days and two nights, following the snakes. Finally, they came to a large cave and the snakes went into the cave, one by one.

Inside the cave, she could see hundreds of pale snakes glowing in the dim light. She walked deeper into the cave until she came up on a large flat rock. On top of the rock was the biggest snake she had seen, fat and coiled. She took a deep breath and said to the snake, "Let my brother go."

The snake replied, "I will let your brother go if you stay as my wife for one year." The girl wanted to heal her brother, so she said yes.

The girl lived as the snake's wife for one year. She hated the dark, cold cave and she hated the things the snake made her do. But after a few months, white scales began to grow on her legs so at least she wasn't so cold.

One year later she said to the giant snake, "I have been your wife for a year. Now I want to go home." The giant snake smiled and said, "But you are my bride, you can't leave me," and he slithered over and wrapped himself around her. The girl was so angry that she grabbed the snake and started tying his body in knots. He cried out and told her to stop but she kept tying him until there were knots all up and down his body and he couldn't slide on the ground anymore. Then she turned and ran as fast out of the cave as fast as she could.

She walked for three days. When she got home, her mother and father were surprised to see her and asked why she had come back. The girl told them, "I stayed for a year so my brother would be cured. The snake didn't want me to leave but I ran away."

The girls' parents asked, "But what if he comes looking for you? Or what if he makes your brother sick again? Maybe you should go back."

The girl didn't want to go back. She wanted to come home to her family. She looked down and saw that her legs still had the pale white scales on them. She tried to shed her snakeskin, but it wouldn't come off.

(The lights change, the music stops, the "fantasy world" ends, and LUISA is left in simple, stark lighting.)

She begged her parents. "Please let me come home. Martín's better now. They won't come looking for me. I know we still have to pay the debt on the land, but we are family, we must stay together." Her parents didn't say anything. And she knew. She knew she couldn't come home.

ALEJANDRA: *(As if seeing her for the first time.)* I'm so sorry, Luisa.

(Starts to cry.)

I'm so sorry...

LUISA: *(Stands up.)* Where did you leave the bike?

(MARCELA sits in the interview area alone.)

MARCELA: I thought I was like Moses, wandering the desert, one of your chosen people. Surviving the cactus and the heat and the spiders and the cold and the snakes and the thorns. Being led into Canaan.

(Pause.)

Imagine this, every day you look around and see people doing bad things. People trying to hurt you and the ones you love. Their government, our government, their police, our police, men in green, men with guns and goggles sitting in lawn chairs, beating us up, shooting us, taking us to jail. And you say, I am not that. I will never be that. Then one day you look at the person standing at your side — your boss, your neighbor, your husband. Your daughter. And you see them betray you. They rob you, they accuse you, they lie to you, they abandon you. But you still think, I am not that. I will never be that. And you believe in yourself, that you're doing the right thing for you and your family and God. So you put your head down and keep going and going until you finally arrive, you finally make it, and you smile and look up. It's completely quiet; you're the only one there. Then you hear the rooster crow twice. And you see who you really are, what you've become.

(Pause.)

I thought you were leading me through the desert. I kept waiting to catch a glimpse of you, to make sure I was going the right way. But the first time I saw you I was going through the windshield.

(Pause.)

I finally saw you, God. And you were laughing.

(MARCELA leaves, is replaced by ALEJANDRA and INTERVIEWER, played by LUISA.)

INTERVIEWER: *Thank you for meeting with me.*

ALEJANDRA: *Of course.*

INTERVIEWER: *How's your leg?*

ALEJANDRA: *It's OK. They're keeping me here another week.*

INTERVIEWER: *(Pause.) I'm just trying to figure out how it all happened.*

ALEJANDRA: *I don't know much. After they left, they found a ride somehow. All packed together when the van went out of control. They think the driver was on drugs or something.*

(Pause.)

I don't know why she rode with him.

INTERVIEWER: *When was the last time you saw her?*

ALEJANDRA: *When we were walking.*

INTERVIEWER: *Why did you split up?*

ALEJANDRA: *I hurt my leg. She and another woman went ahead.*

INTERVIEWER: *That must have been hard.*

ALEJANDRA: *It was. I was scared. And angry.*

INTERVIEWER: *No, I mean it must have been hard to get her to go. She'd never leave anyone in the desert. After what happened to her.*

(Long pause.)

She'd never leave anyone.

(Silence.)

ALEJANDRA: *(Makes a decision.) I told her there was no use in all of us dying. I told her I'd be fine, that she should call for help when she got to the road. She didn't want to. I had to make her go. I had to force her.*

INTERVIEWER: *That's her. That's exactly her.*

(Starts crying.)

You know the last time I saw her?

ALEJANDRA: What?

INTERVIEWER: The last time I saw her, I — I was getting off a bus. She was there waiting for me but some Border Patrol were talking to her. I walked right past her. Didn't look at her. Like she wasn't even there. I can't believe it. The last time I'd ever see her and I didn't even —

ALEJANDRA: It's OK. It's all right. She knew.

(ALEJANDRA hugs her as she cries.)

She knew. It's OK. That's what she wanted you...she knew.

(ALEJANDRA consoles INTERVIEWER until she calms down.)

ALEJANDRA: So what are you going to do now?

INTERVIEWER: I'm going home.

ALEJANDRA: Houston?

INTERVIEWER: No, home.

ALEJANDRA: You're leaving? But you can get papers now, why would you leave? This is what she wanted. For you to be here and have a better life. To go to school, buy a house —

INTERVIEWER: I know.

ALEJANDRA: — get a job, get married, raise kids and not worry about how to feed them, not worry about anything.

INTERVIEWER: I don't laugh here. I don't laugh the way I did at home.

> *(Pause.)*

I hate this country. I hate it. It takes something from you. Everyone treats you like an animal and you start believing they're right. I don't want to be in a place like this. I don't want to be in a place that makes me pretend I don't know my own mother.

> *(Pause.)*

No one should ever have to do that.

> *(Silence.)*

INTERVIEWER: (To ALEJANDRA.) So what are you going to do?

(Silence, ALEJANDRA thinks. Music starts, lights shift.)

INTERVIEWER: *In the night sky, the skeleton flew south. It landed in front of a house that was guarded by a lioness. The lioness took the skeleton inside. The skeleton set a woman's head on the ground, lit a candle, and began to sing. As it was singing, the head rolled up the side of the bed, put itself back on its body, and opened its eyes. They looked at each other for a moment, then the skeleton left the house and flew away.*

(Lights down. End of play.)

Borderlands Theater

Borderlands Theater is a professional theater company recognized nationally and internationally for the development and production of theater and educational programs that reflect the diversity of voices of the US / Mexico border region. Although focusing on the Latino(a) / Chicano(a) voice as the core voice to nurture and support, Borderlands works interactively with all of the voices of the region.

The "border," both as physical and social landscape, is a metaphor for Borderlands' work. The metaphor allows, invites and even demands, both a regional and an international understanding of what it represents. Border people, in the best sense of the world, are citizens of the world.

Borderlands was founded in 1986.

Barclay Goldsmith, Producing Director

Borderlands Theater
Tucson, Arizona

Website: http://www.borderlandstheater.org

NoPassport

NoPassport is a Pan-American theatre alliance & press devoted to live, virtual and print action, advocacy and change toward the fostering of cross-cultural diversity in the arts with an emphasis on the embrace of the hemispheric spirit in US Latina/o and Latin-American theatre-making.

NoPassport Press' Dreaming the Americas Series and Theatre & Performance PlayTexts Series promotes new writing for the stage, texts on theory and practice and theatrical translations.

Series Editors:
Randy Gener, Jorge Huerta, Otis RamseyZoe, Stephen Squibb, Caridad Svich

Advisory Board:
Daniel Banks, Amparo Garcia-Crow, Maria M. Delgado, Elana Greenfield, Christina Marin, Antonio Ocampo Guzman, Sarah Cameron Sunde, Saviana Stanescu, Tamara Underiner, Patricia Ybarra

NoPassport is a sponsored project of Fractured Atlas, a non-profit arts service organization. Contributions in behalf of [Caridad Svich & NoPassport] may be made payable to Fractured Atlas and are tax-deductible to the extent permitted

by law. For online donations go directly to
https://www.fracturedatlas.org/donate/2623

MORE TITLES AVAILABLE FROM NoPASSPORT PRESS

Antigone Project: A Play in Five Parts
by Tanya Barfield, Karen Hartman, Chiori Miyagawa, Lynn
Nottage and Caridad Svich, with preface by Lisa Schlesinger,
introduction by Marianne McDonald
ISBN 978-0-578-03150-7

Migdalia Cruz: El Grito del Bronx & other plays
(Salt, Yellow Eyes, El Grito del Bronx, Da Bronx rocks: a song)
Introduction by Alberto Sandoval-Sanchez,
afterword by Priscilla Page
ISBN: 978-0-578-04992-2

Amparo Garcia-Crow: The South Texas Plays
(Cocks Have Claws and Wings to Fly, Under a Western Sky,
The Faraway Nearby, Esmeralda Blue); Preface by Octavio
Solis
ISBN: 978-0-578-01913-0

Anne Garcia-Romero: Collected Plays
(Earthquake Chica, Santa Concepcion, Mary Peabody in Cuba)
Preface by Juliette Carrillo
ISBN: 978-0-6151-8888-1

Girl Under Grain by Karen Hartman
introduction by Jean Randich
ISBN: 978-0-578-04981-6

**John Jesurun: Deep Sleep, White Water, Black Maria
– A Media Trilogy** ; Preface by Fiona Templeton
ISBN: 978-0-578-02602-2

Lorca: Six Major Plays
(Blood Wedding, Dona Rosita, The House of Bernarda Alba,
The Public, The Shoemaker's Prodigious Wife, Yerma)

*In new translations by Caridad Svich, Preface by James
Leverett, introduction by Amy Rogoway, ISBN: 978-0-578-
00221-7*

Matthew Maguire: Three Plays
*(The Tower, Luscious Music, The Desert); Preface by Naomi
Wallace*
ISBN: 978-0-578-00856-1

Octavio Solis: The River Plays
(El Otro, Dreamlandia,Bethlehem);
introduction by Douglas Langworthy
ISBN: 978-0-578-04881-9

Oliver Mayer: Collected Plays
(Conjunto, Joe Louis Blues, Ragged Time)
 Preface by Luis Alfaro, Introduction by Jon D. Rossini
ISBN: 978-0-6151-8370-1

Alejandro Morales: Collected Plays
(expat/inferno, marea, Sebastian)
ISBN: 978-0-6151-8621-4

Saviana Stanescu: The New York Plays
(Waxing West, Lenin's Shoe, Aliens with Extraordinary Skills)
introduction by John Clinton Eisner
ISBN: 978-0-578-04942-7

12 Ophelias (a play with broken songs) by Caridad Svich
ISBN: 978-0-6152-4918-6

Woman Killer by Chiori Miyagawa
introduction by Sharon Friedman,
afterword by Martin Harries
ISBN: 978-0-578-05008-9

The Tropic of X by Caridad Svich
Introduction by Marvin Carlson,
Afterword by Tamara Underiner
ISBN: 978-0-578-03871-1

CPSIA information can be obtained at www.ICGtesting.com
Printed in the USA
LVOW07s0253080714

393313LV00002B/130/P